Amazing
Snakes

EYEWITNESS JUNIORS

Amazing
Snakes

WRITTEN BY
ALEXANDRA PARSONS

PHOTOGRAPHED BY
JERRY YOUNG

ALFRED A. KNOPF • NEW YORK

Editor Scott Steedman
Designers Ann Cannings and Margo Beamish-White
Senior art editor Jacquie Gulliver
Editorial director Sue Unstead
Art director Anne-Marie Bulat

Special photography by Jerry Young
Illustrations by Colin Woolf and Jane Gedye
Animals supplied by Trevor Smith's Animal World
Editorial consultants
The staff of the Natural History Museum, London

This is a Borzoi Book published by Alfred A. Knopf, Inc.

This Eyewitness Junior Book has been conceived, edited, and
designed by Dorling Kindersley Limited

First American edition, 1990

Manufactured in Spain   19 18 17 16 15

Library of Congress Cataloging in Publication Data
Parsons, Alexandra
Amazing snakes / written by Alexandra Parsons;
photographs by Jerry Young.
p. cm. — (Eyewitness juniors)
Summary: Text and photographs introduce amazing members of
the snake world, including the sunbeam snake, milk snake, and
reticulated python.
1. Snakes — Juvenile literature. [1. Snakes.] I. Young, Jerry, ill.
II. Title. III. Series: Parsons, Alexandra. Eyewitness juniors.
QL666.06P34   1990   597.96 — dc20   89-38944
ISBN 0-679-80225-8
ISBN 0-679-90225-2 (lib. bdg.)

Color reproduction by Colourscan, Singapore
Typeset by Windsorgraphics, Ringwood, Hampshire
Printed in Spain by Artes Gráficas Toledo, S.A.
D.L.TO:1296-1998

Contents

What is a snake? 8

The sunbeam snake 10

The big squeeze 12

The egg eater 14

The deadly cobra 16

The rattlesnake 18

The milk snake 20

A snake that flies? 22

The tree boa 24

The vine snake 26

How snakes move 28

Index 29

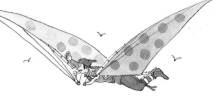

What is a snake?

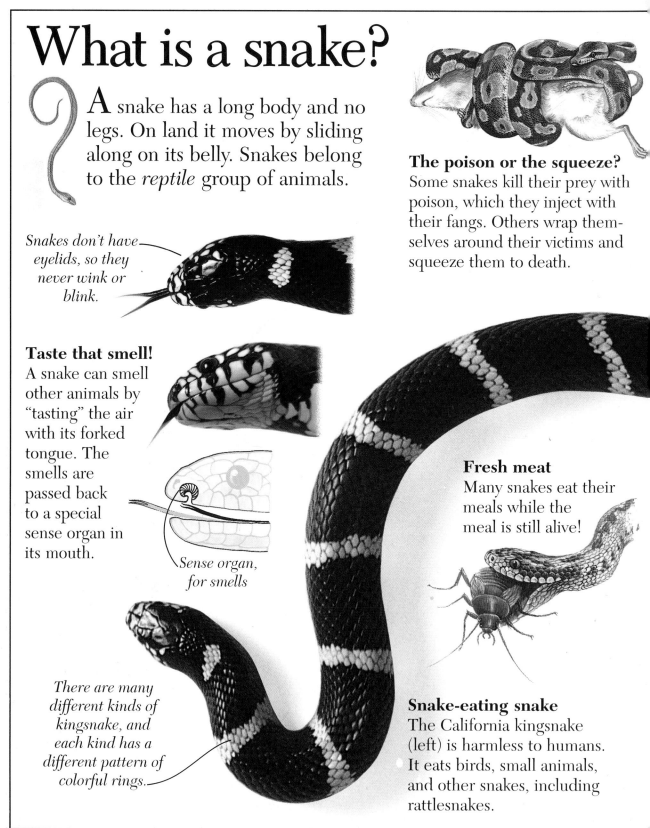

A snake has a long body and no legs. On land it moves by sliding along on its belly. Snakes belong to the *reptile* group of animals.

The poison or the squeeze?
Some snakes kill their prey with poison, which they inject with their fangs. Others wrap themselves around their victims and squeeze them to death.

Snakes don't have eyelids, so they never wink or blink.

Taste that smell!
A snake can smell other animals by "tasting" the air with its forked tongue. The smells are passed back to a special sense organ in its mouth.

Sense organ, for smells

Fresh meat
Many snakes eat their meals while the meal is still alive!

There are many different kinds of kingsnake, and each kind has a different pattern of colorful rings.

Snake-eating snake
The California kingsnake (left) is harmless to humans. It eats birds, small animals, and other snakes, including rattlesnakes.

The big swallow

Snakes can't chew their food before they eat it, so they have to swallow their victims whole. Their jawbones are held together by ligaments which work like rubber bands, so they can open their mouths very wide.

Snake bones

Snakes have very long backbones and so many ribs you'd lose track trying to count them all.

Sshh!

Snakes don't have outer ears. They "feel" sounds by picking up vibrations in the ground.

Snakes have very complicated joints in their backbones which allow them to bend in almost any direction.

The sunbeam snake

The sunbeam snake has beautiful skin that shimmers in the sunlight. But it spends most of its day hidden underground, and comes out at sundown to hunt for food.

The sunbeam snake lives in the rice paddies of China and Indonesia.

Snake skin
A snake's skin is made up of hundreds of tiny scales which overlap like tiles on a roof.

Friendly fellows
There are 2,700 different kinds of snakes in the world, divided into 30 family groups. Most of them are harmless to humans.

Long, cool, and dry
Snakes aren't wet and slimy. Their skin is actually dry and cool. It only looks wet because it shines in the light.

Shedding skin

All that sliding wears out a snake's skin. So several times a year the snake crawls out of its old skin, revealing a shiny new layer that has grown underneath.

Molting starts at the snake's head.

A snake's shadow

A snake may molt, or shed its skin, in one complete piece. When it does this, it leaves behind an eerie, see-through, inside-out image of its body.

A winter snooze

In places where it gets cold in the winter, snakes "sleep" during the cold months. This is called hibernating. Some snakes hibernate in caves; others spend the winter underground.

The big squeeze

The reticulate python is one of the biggest, longest, strongest snakes in the world. It is not poisonous, but it can squeeze the life out of a small deer.

Catch me if you can

There are reports of pythons eating people, but this happens very rarely. Few snakes are big enough to swallow a human, and really big snakes are so fat and slow they'd be very lucky to catch one!

King size

Ask a grown-up to take 10 giant steps, and mark where he or she starts and finishes. That should be about 33 feet, the length of the longest python. It was found in the jungles of Thailand in Asia.

A very solid snake
The heaviest snake in the world is the anaconda. A large anaconda can have a body as thick as a barrel and weigh 400 pounds – that's as heavy as three adults.

A python is patterned to match the leaves on the forest floor.

Squeeze me
A python can squeeze the life out of a goat or a wild pig in less than a minute.

Snake hips
Pythons are descended from prehistoric lizards that lived at the same time as the dinosaurs. They still have tiny, useless "spurs" where their hips and legs used to be.

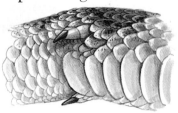

Gulp!
Would you believe that a python can swallow a whole goat? Well, it can. The snake doesn't chew or swallow the way we do. It simply moves its body forward with its jaws wide open and "walks" the animal down its throat.

The egg eater

There is a group of snakes that eats nothing but birds' eggs. They swallow the egg whole, squash it, ingest the insides, and spit out the shell.

Stretchy skin
The egg eater is slim, with very stretchy skin that won't burst if the snake swallows a huge egg.

Night worker
This egg-eating snake comes from Africa. It sleeps during the day and searches for eggs at night.

special spikes

backbone

Toothless
An egg-eating snake doesn't have many teeth, so it will not break the egg by accident while swallowing it.

Sawbones
The egg eater has a row of special sharp spikes that stick down from the back of its throat. Once it has swallowed an egg, the snake bends its head down, pushing the egg up against these spikes. This cuts a slit in the egg-shell so that the insides come out.

The egg-eating snake can swallow a bird's egg twice the size of its head.

Lazybones
Like some people, snakes move only if they are hot, hungry, or frightened. Otherwise they move very little all day long.

Squish squash
Getting rid of the eggshell is very hard work. The snake tightens its muscles to crush the shell and then spits it out in a nice neat bundle. The whole egg-eating process takes about 15 minutes.

before   *after*

The deadly cobra

Of all the snakes in the world, the cobra is one of the most frightening. Cobra poison is very strong – a bite from a cobra could kill a human in 15 minutes.

Short-tempered snake
The cobra is quick to attack. When it senses danger, it lifts the front of its body off the ground, spreads its hood, and hisses like mad.

What a mover!
The cobra is one of the few snakes in the world that can move forward while the upper part of its body is raised off the ground.

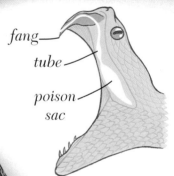

fang

tube

poison sac

Poison sacs
Deadly poisonous snakes have big poison sacs on each side of their head. Little tubes run from each poison sac to the fangs.

A scary story

The Greeks have a legend about a terrible monster named Medusa who had snakes instead of hair. She was so ugly that anyone who looked at her was turned to stone. A brave and clever hero named Perseus, using his shiny shield as a mirror, managed to lop off Medusa's head without looking at her hideous face.

A sad story

Long ago there was a beautiful queen of Egypt named Cleopatra who was very sad because the man she loved had died. She killed herself by letting one of the royal cobras bite her.

Dangerous babies

Cobras can bite and kill as soon as they are born. Just one tablespoon of their poison – even dried – could kill 165 people or over 160,000 mice.

How charming!

Snake charmers can make snakes dance to their music. At least that's what it looks like. In fact, the snake can't even hear the music and is just copying the swaying movements of the charmer and the flute.

Don't spit!

"Spitting" cobras, found in Africa, don't really spit. When they feel threatened, they spray jets of poison into their attacker's eyes.

The rattlesnake

The rattler is one of the fastest killers in the animal world. It strikes at a speed of 10 feet per second, and its poison is deadly.

Its scaly, patterned skin makes the rattlesnake hard to see when it is coiled up under a pile of leaves.

Baby snakes

Unlike most snakes, which lay eggs, rattlers give birth to live young. As soon as they are born, the mother leaves and they are on their own.

Rattle, rattle

The rattler gets its name from the rattling sound made by the rings on its tail. Each time the snake sheds its skin, a new ring is added. When the snake wants to frighten its enemies, it shakes its rattle very fast.

Each time a rattlesnake sheds its skin, a new ring is added to the tail. The rings are made of the same substance as your toenails.

Pajama party

Rattlesnakes gather in groups to sleep through the winter. Sometimes up to 1,000 of them will coil up together.

What a job!

Snake poison, also called venom, is an important ingredient in some medicines. To collect the venom, people who have been specially trained for the job "milk" the snakes – very, very carefully!

Look out!

Rattlesnakes are the most dangerous snakes in America. They bite people only if they are stepped on, however, so if you are walking around in the desert, watch where you put your feet!

The milk snake

This is one of the most colorful snakes in the world. It is not poisonous. It eats mice and birds, which it kills by squeezing.

The milk snake lives and hunts under logs and rotting leaves.

coral snake

Confusing colors

The milk snake looks a lot like the deadly coral snake, which has stripes of the same color but in a different order. Here is a little rhyme to help you tell which is which:

Red to yellow, kill a fellow,
Red to black, venom lack.

Blending in

Some snakes are very well camouflaged. This means that their patterns blend in with the background so that enemies find it hard to see them.

Unlucky for some

Milk snakes lay about 13 eggs – in piles of animal manure.

egg tooth

Let me out!

Baby snakes get out of their eggs all by themselves. They have a special little "egg tooth" to saw through the shell.

Does it drink milk?

No, it doesn't. People used to think that the milk snake sneaked into cowsheds to suck milk from cows. It does sneak into cowsheds, but it is looking for mice, not milk.

Keep reading

A snake expert is called a herpetologist (HER-puh-TAHL-uh-jist). That's what you will be when you finish reading this book.

The world's smallest snake

This honor goes to the rare thread snake of the West Indies. If you could take the lead out of a pencil, the tiny thread snake could slither through the hole.

A snake that flies?

In the hot and steamy jungles of Asia lives the amazing flying snake. This beautiful animal can leap into the air and glide from tree to tree.

The flying snake takes off by uncoiling quickly, like a spring.

Bats for breakfast
A flying snake enjoys a diet of lizards, birds, frogs, and bats, which it kills with poison and then swallows head first.

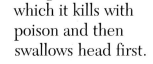

ribs

Flat out
Flying snakes glide through the air by pushing out their ribs and holding in their bellies until they are flat like a ribbon.

Skydiving

Flying snakes don't really fly. They glide through the air in a giant S-shape.

The rough scales on the snake's belly help it to climb trees.

When danger strikes

Flying snakes don't take off too often – only when they are in danger of attack from hawks or eagles soaring overhead.

Looping the loop

The flying snake can only "fly" downward or across, not up. But it can steer in the air by twisting its body back and forth.

The tree boa

These impressive-looking snakes live in the jungles of South America. They hunt by "feeling" the heat from their victims' bodies, and kill by squeezing.

Fearsome fangs
The tree boa's closed mouth hides its long, sharp front teeth – good for catching fast-moving birds and bats.

Where's my lunch?
The hungry tree boa hangs from branches and swings its head from side to side. When it feels the same amount of heat on both sides, it knows that a meal is right in front of it.

Monkey business
The tree boa uses its strong tail to grab on to branches in the same way a monkey does. It can hold more than half of its body suspended in midair.

Flying meal
All kinds of small creatures can end up on a boa's dinner menu, from bats to rats. The emerald tree boa (below) even snatches birds on the wing.

Bath night
Tree boas leave their trees only to take a swim in a jungle river or go for a quick slither in a swamp.

heat spots

Like many snakes that live in trees, Cook's tree boa is lightly colored on its belly and dark on top. From above it blends in with the forest floor, and from below with the sky.

Hunting for warmth

Even in total darkness, the boa can tell if there is a nice meal hiding nearby. It has little holes on its lips that can "feel" an animal's body heat.

Hanging loose

A tree boa doesn't coil itself around its branch. Instead, it just flops over the branch in loops, ready to straighten out and hurl itself at a victim.

Poached or fried?

If you ever find yourself dining out with Indians in South America's Amazon jungle, don't be surprised if they serve you a slice or two of tree boa.

The vine snake

The vine snake lies very still in its tree, waiting for something tasty to pass by. Wrapped around a branch, it looks like a harmless piece of jungle vine.

Watching and waiting

The vine snake has very good eyesight. Both of its eyes face forward, like human eyes, so the snake can judge distances as it goes in for the kill. Its head is long and pointed, like the nose of a fighter plane.

A vine snake may grow longer than your leg, but it will never get much fatter than your finger.

Thirsty?

Snakes that live in trees, like the vine snake, drink dew and rain-water from leaves. Snakes that live on the ground get their water from grass and puddles of rain.

Quick as a wink

The vine snake may stay still for hours and hours, but when it finally moves, it is as fast as lightning. It can snatch a bird or a lizard in a third of a second. That's about the time it takes to blink.

Killer juices

The digestive juices of most snakes are so strong they can turn bones into mush.

Most trees are green, and so are most tree-dwelling snakes.

Back teeth

The vine snake has fangs at the back of its mouth, so it can give its lunch a jab of poison on the way down. Deadlier snakes, such as cobras, have fangs at the very front of their mouths.

poison sac

fangs

How snakes move

Moving along without legs or arms could be a little difficult, but snakes have found a way. In fact, they have found several ways.

Sidewinding
This "sidestepping" movement is ideal for soft sand, which is hard to grip. From an S-shaped position on the ground, the snake flicks its head a few feet to one side. Then it pulls the rest of its body up to its head to form another S-shape – ready to start again.

Cool belly
When moving like this, the snake's belly hardly touches the hot sand. This is one reason why some desert snakes get around by sidewinding. This sidewinder is found in the scorching deserts of the West.

Not so fast
Don't worry – you could easily outrun a snake. Snakes don't move very fast and they get tired quickly. The fastest ones can slither along at about the same speed as a person walking, but they cannot keep up the pace for more than a few minutes.

Concertina
This movement is good for tight spots. The snake bunches up its body in loops and then straightens out, pushing its head forward. Then it pulls its tail up to join the rest of the body.

Wriggling
To wriggle, the snake pushes against rocks or other hard objects, first on one side and then on the other. Its body seems to move forward in waves.

When a snake is creeping, its body is almost straight. All you can see are ripples running down its back.

Creeping
Fat snakes, like pythons, can creep along. They slide their skin back and forth, gripping with their belly scales

Index

anaconda 13

bones 9

camouflage 13, 20, 25
Cleopatra 17
cobra 16–17, 27
concertina 29
Cook's tree boa 25
coral snake 20
creeping 29

ears 9
egg-eating snake 14–15
eggs 18, 21
egg tooth 21
eyesight 26

fangs 8, 16, 25, 27
flying snake 22–23

heat spots 25
herpetologist 21
hibernating 11, 19

kingsnake, Californian 8–9

Medusa 17
milk snake 20–21
movement 28–29

Perseus 17
poison 8, 16, 17, 18, 19, 22
poison sacs 16, 27

rattlesnake 18–19
reticulate python 12–13

scales 10, 23
sidewinder 28
skin 10, 11, 14
skin, shedding of 11
snake charmers 17
snakes: heaviest 13;
  longest 12; smallest 21
spitting cobra 17
squeezing 8, 12, 13, 20
sunbeam snake 10–11
swallowing 9, 13

tree boa 24–25

vine snake 26–27

wriggling 29